MW00889499

CHAPTER 1

THE RUSHED GAMER

Once upon a time, playing a magical game called "Mystic Builders," there was a boy named Gavin. Gavin loved to make big, amazing things in the game. He dreamed of castles reaching high into the sky and towns bustling with life.

But Gavin had a problem. He always rushed. Whenever he started building something new, like a big castle or a cozy house, he hurried and didn't think much about where he put each block.

He wanted to see his creations right away, but because he rushed, they often fell down. His buildings were not strong, and Gavin felt sad when they crumbled.

CHAPTER 2

THE ANCIENT TURTLE'S ADVICE

One day, while Gavin was trying to build again, he met a wise turtle in the game. The turtle looked at Gavin with friendly eyes and said, "Hey there, young builder.

If you want to make something amazing, you need to be patient." Gavin listened carefully as the turtle spoke. "Great things take time," the turtle said softly."You have to plan carefully and work slowly. If you do that, your dreams will come true."

Gavin thought about what the turtle said. Maybe rushing wasn't helping him at all.

CHAPTER 3

A CASTLE WORTH THE WAIT

Deciding to listen to the turtle's advice, Gavin began to build again. This time, he took his time. He thought about where each block should go and chose the best ones for his castle.

Brick by brick, stone by stone, Gavin worked hard on his creation. Even though it took a long time, he didn't give up. After many days of patient work, Gavin finally finished his castle.

It was strong and beautiful, standing tall and proud in the game world. Gavin felt so happy and proud of what he had made.

CHAPTER 4

PATIENCE IN PRACTICE

Gavin was so excited about his castle that he decided to tell his friends. He wrote a book called "The Castle That Patience Built" to share his story.

When he went back to school, he read his book to his classmates. He told them how being patient helped him make something amazing.

As Gavin spoke, he saw his friends' eyes light up with excitement. They wanted to try being patient too, just like Gavin. Together, they learned that with patience and hard work, they could do anything they set their minds to.

HARD WORK

And so, they set off on new adventures, ready to build and create with patience and determination.

Questions for discussion:

1. What was Gavin's favorite thing to do in the game "Mystic Builders"?
2. Why did Gavin's buildings keep falling down?
3. What advice did the wise turtle give Gavin?

Gavin's Digital Adventures: Lessons Beyond the Screen
3 book series

Book 1: Gavin and the Quest of Teamwork

Book 2: Gavin's Adventure of Patience

Book 3: Gavin and the Challenge of Empathy

For Parents:

Restorative practices are a way of solving problems that focus on healing and fixing relationships instead of just punishing someone when they do something wrong. It's like having a conversation to understand everyone's feelings and needs when there's a conflict or issue.

This method helps everyone involved to listen to each other, express their feelings, and work together to find a fair solution. For parents, this means teaching kids to talk about their problems, understand how their actions affect others, and learn how to make things right.

This approach helps build a caring and respectful family environment where everyone feels heard and valued.

Made in the USA
Las Vegas, NV
12 March 2024

87109274R00015